To Charlie,
Abby & Lilah

Christmas 2009

Much Love -
Grandma & Grandpa
xo xo xo

Merry Christmas

A Canadian Keepsake Collection

Scholastic Canada Ltd.
Toronto New York London Auckland Sydney
Mexico City New Delhi Hong Kong Buenos Aires

Scholastic Canada Ltd.
604 King Street West, Toronto, Ontario M5V 1E1, Canada

Scholastic Inc.
557 Broadway, New York, NY 10012, USA

Scholastic Australia Pty Limited
PO Box 579, Gosford, NSW 2250, Australia

Scholastic New Zealand Limited
Private Bag 94407, Greenmount, Auckland, New Zealand

Scholastic Children's Books
Euston House, 24 Eversholt Street, London NW1 1DB, UK

Library and Archives Canada Cataloguing in Publication

Merry Christmas : a Canadian keepsake collection

Contents:
Little crooked Christmas tree / Michael Cutting ;
illustrated by Ron Broda — Sadie the ballerina / Joan Betty
Stuchner ; illustrated by Bruno St-Aubin — Moon and
star / Robin Muller — One special tree / Olena
Kassian —Woodland Christmas / Frances Tyrrell.
ISBN 978-0-545-98667-0

1. Christmas stories, Canadian (English).   2. Children's
stories, Canadian (English).   I. Title.

PS8237.C57M47 2009   jC813'.0108334   C2009-902339-3

ISBN-10 0-545-98667-2

6 5 4 3 2 1   Printed in Singapore   09 10 11 12 13

Contents

The Little Crooked Christmas Tree

Michael Cutting   Ron Broda

To Tasha, whose love of nature
made this story possible.
M.C.

To my mother, Jean Broda.
Love, Number Six.
R.B.

The Little
Crooked Christmas Tree

Story by **Michael Cutting**

Paper sculptures by **Ron Broda**

Out beyond the town, where the farms begin, is an unusual field. In the early spring, when all the other fields are bare and brown, this field is green and bright because it is filled with little Christmas trees. This is the story of one special tree.

From where the little tree was growing, among the rows and rows of trees, he could at last see the big, bold letters of the sign that had puzzled him for so long. There it stood, at the end of the field —"Brown's Christmas Tree Farm."

He was sure that he was a tree, but he didn't know what a Christmas tree was, or even what Christmas was. He did know that he was supposed to grow straight and tall and healthy for some special reason.

Every few days a man would walk past and look at him. The man would pull out the weeds around his trunk and spray him all over, getting rid of the itchy bugs and the pesky caterpillars that clogged up his needles and nibbled at his bark.

By the time he was seven years old, the little tree was big enough for birds and other creatures to perch on his branches. He looked forward to the arrival of such new visitors in the hope that they would be able to answer his questions about Christmas.

His first visitor was a goose, who stopped to nibble the fresh young grass by his trunk. "Please, Miss Goose," asked the tree, "what is Christmas? And what is a Christmas tree?"

"You're asking the wrong bird," said the goose. "My friends and I always go south at that time of the year."

Soon a squirrel came by, leaping from tree to tree. "Please, Mr. Squirrel, what is a Christmas tree? And what is Christmas?"

"You're asking the wrong squirrel," he said. "We always sleep through that time of year."

Then one stormy day a white dove came to rest on his topmost branch. It landed with a thump, fell off one branch through the next and the next, until the tree pulled his softest branches together to make a thick, green bed that caught and cradled the little white dove.

"Oh, thank you, little tree," said the white dove. "I'm just too, too tired to fly any further. Strong winds blew me away from my home. The beautiful nest I worked so hard on was blown right off the tree, and it's time for me to lay my eggs. Oh, little tree, can you pull your softest branches together and hold them like that as a nest for my eggs?"

For weeks and weeks the little tree struggled to keep his branches close and still as the eggs hatched and three baby doves peeped and cooed. While the busy mother dove was out hunting for seeds, the little tree made an even greater effort and pulled his branches right over them to shelter them from the sun and the rain and hide them from hawks and other dangerous creatures.

The little tree worked so hard helping the white dove raise her children, always pulling his branches over to one side, that he forgot all about growing straight and tall as a Christmas tree should. Gradually he developed a big hump in his trunk.

The farmer walked past and looked disappointed, and he shook his head sadly. He stopped pulling out the weeds around the little tree's trunk. He hardly bothered to spray him for itchy bugs or nibbling caterpillars any more. The little tree felt quite neglected, but he would not give up taking care of the white dove and her children.

The day arrived when the little doves were big enough to learn to fly. They stretched their wings and flapped all the way to the next tree and back. Gradually they began to fly further and further, but they always came back to the little tree at dusk.

One day the mother dove said to the tree, "Oh, little tree, by saving my life and taking care of my children you've grown a big hump in your trunk. The farmer hardly bothers to pull out the weeds around you or spray your branches anymore, and it's all my fault."

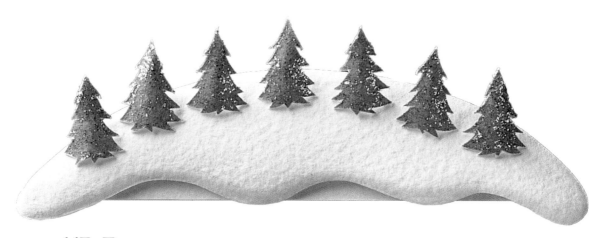

"Now it's time for us to fly back to the big tree where I once lived. The people in the house nearby put out seeds every day in the winter for me, as they did for my mother and grandmother before me. It's so hard to find food when the ground is covered in snow, and besides, I'm sure they miss us. But I promise we'll all be back to visit with you in the spring. Tell me, is there anything I can do for you before we go?"

"Please, Mrs. Dove," cried the little tree, "before you go, can you tell me what a Christmas tree is, and what Christmas is? I know that I'll never be a proper Christmas tree now, but I would still like to know what I might have been, and what all the trees I grew up with are going to be."

"Little tree," said the dove, "Christmas is a time when people celebrate the birth of Jesus Christ, who was born to bring peace to the world. Just before Christmas, families bring their children to find a nice, straight Christmas tree. They cut it down and take it home, where it is decorated with coloured lights and shiny ornaments, and they place gifts around it. Grandparents and aunts and uncles and friends all come to admire the tree. Then, when the holiday is over, the lights and ornaments are put away and the poor tree is thrown out, alone, in the snow. By saving me and my children you have grown crooked, but now you are safe."

The snow came, the winds howled, the pond froze. The
birds flew south, the squirrels slept, nothing and no one
moved on Brown's Christmas Tree Farm.

Then one day, with the snow softly falling, the field
was filled with people. Mothers, fathers, children, all
laughing and talking, all looking for the perfect tree to take
home. Some even looked at the little tree, but when they
brushed the snow from his branches and saw the hump on
his trunk, they shook their heads and moved on.

But along with the laughter, the thud of axes and the
sound of splitting wood filled the air. The little tree stood
helpless as one by one all the other trees fell and were
dragged away to the waiting cars.

That was the loneliest time of the tree's life. All that long, cold winter he stood alone with nothing to shelter him from the icy winds. When the spring came, no birds stopped by, for one lonely, crooked tree in an empty field was no place to rest on their long journey. Farmer Brown came out with some men, who planted hundreds of baby Christmas trees in rows up and down the field. No one took any notice of the little tree, except to hang their coats on his branches.

One warm and sunny morning, there was a gentle cooing and a flapping of wings. The white dove had kept her promise and had brought her children back to visit.

"Oh, I missed you so much," sobbed the little tree. "I thought that winter had taken you from me. Oh, Mrs. Dove, I'm so alone. They cut down all the friends I grew up with and took them away. No one wanted me because of the hump on my trunk. Nobody was left to shelter me from the icy winds. Farmer Brown planted rows of baby trees, but they're far too young for me to talk to. You told me that a Christmas tree only has coloured lights and shiny ornaments for a short time, but I'd rather bring happiness and laughter to children for those special few days than be lonely and cold all winter by myself. Isn't that what I was made for, to be a symbol of joy and love?"

The white dove and her children comforted the little tree. They stayed with him all day, and flew off with a promise to return soon.

Summer came, and one day Farmer Brown arrived with some men, some shovels and a strange machine. They dug and dug and dug all around the little tree's roots. They wrapped them in damp sacking, then used the machine to lift him carefully out of the ground and onto a truck.

It was a long journey lying on his side, with the sun drying his roots and making him thirsty. Eventually the truck arrived at a big house, where a deep hole was waiting in the garden, just the shape and size of the little tree's roots. They lifted him carefully from the truck, undid the sacking, placed him in the hole and filled in the earth around him. Then they soaked the ground with cool, fresh water. The little tree sighed and settled his roots gratefully.

The next day, he looked around at his new home. All kinds of strange flowers grew nearby. The grass was even and green, not tufted with the brown patches that he was used to. But, strangest of all, he was surrounded by the most unusual trees. The little Christmas tree had never seen anything like them. He was positively dwarfed by them! Some grew in clumps, others towered alone to the sky, and some even had flowers on their branches. There wasn't another Christmas tree in sight.

Nevertheless, it was nice to be with trees again, so he plucked up his courage and spoke to one. "Excuse me, sir. I'm a Christmas tree. Who are you?"

"Harrumph," replied the haughty birch. "You're not a real tree. You're just a scrubby little spruce with a crooked trunk and prickly needles. A real tree has silver bark and soft green leaves. You don't belong in this garden." With that, he turned his leaves to the sun and ignored the little tree.

Timidly, the little tree turned his branches up and spoke to the giant behind him. "Excuse me, sir. I just arrived last night. I'm a Christmas tree. Who are you?"

"By my acorns," thundered the proud oak, "real trees grow straight and tall. You're not a real tree. You're just a crooked little nothing."

And so it was with all the others. They wouldn't speak to him because he wasn't tall enough, or straight enough, or wearing the right colour bark. The little Christmas tree was just as lonely as he had been in the empty field. Even the birds ignored him, preferring to perch in the branches of the taller trees.

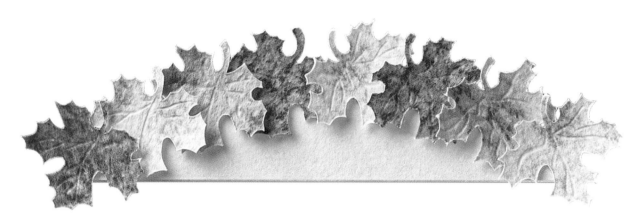

As summer turned to autumn and nights became cold, all the trees started to change. Their greens turned to golds and browns. Leaves hung limply from branches and then fell to the ground. The giant oak shivered naked in the winter winds. The haughty birch, whose bark was not quite as fine when there were no leaves to hide it, shook in the sleet and rain. The only one who stood green and fresh in the garden was the little Christmas tree.

Even as autumn turned to winter, and the rain turned to snow, the little tree stood proudly green and fresh, with a lacy coat of fluffy white snow on his branches.

One cold day the people of the house came out to the little tree with big boxes full of beautiful things. They hung strings and strings of coloured lights from his branches, and they decorated him from top to bottom with shiny ornaments and bright ribbons.

The little tree stood as tall and proud as he could. He stretched and strained and tried to stand straight and tall. But with his coloured lights glowing and his shiny ornaments glittering, no one seemed to notice that he was little and crooked. People stopped their cars to admire him. The children of the house checked his lights and ornaments daily to make sure that none had blown off.

On Christmas Eve, the people of the house came out, bundled against the cold. People arrived from all around the neighbourhood. Even strangers stopped to join. Softly, sweetly, they sang in harmony.

O holy night, the stars are brightly shining,
This is the night of our dear saviour's birth.

As the last notes died away in the still night, there was a cooing and a whirring of wings. The people looked up and saw, perched on the very tip of the little tree, a beautiful white dove.

The dove remained on top of the tree until the last neighbour had left and the last child had gone to sleep. Then she slipped closer in among the branches and said softly, "Little Christmas tree, you gave me shelter when I was too tired to fly any further. You gave me your softest branches as a nest for my children. In doing this you caused yourself to grow crooked, and you suffered through a long, cold, lonely winter."

"When we parted, you asked me about Christmas trees, and about the meaning of Christmas. Even then, after seeing the fate of all your friends, you wanted to fulfil your destiny.

"Look down, little tree. Look at your branches. See the shiny ornaments, see the bright lights, see the footprints in the snow of all the people who came to admire you. This is your reward. For many years to come, you will stand proudly in this garden, and every Christmas you will be decorated like this and surrounded by love."

The little tree looked down. He saw himself shining in the dark. He saw the footprints in the snow of all the people who had come to share their joy around him. And he felt bigger and taller than any tree that garden had ever seen.

Thanks to Rick Welch.
This book is for Tom and Dov and for
all my stage-struck young friends,
especially Naomi Vogt and
Yamit Shem-Tov. Break a leg!
— J.B.S.

Claude and Zoé,
my two favorite ballerinas.
— B.S-A.

Sadie the Ballerina

Joan Betty Stuchner   Bruno St-Aubin

Sadie wanted to be a ballerina. She pictured her name in lights on a theatre marquee: *Sadie Levine Dancing Tonight!*

"I'm a natural," she said.
She waved her arms.
She pointed her toes.
She tilted her head.
She tripped on the rug and fell on her bed.

But she didn't give up.
"Practise makes perfect," she said.

She twirled and tripped again.

Sadie watched ballet on television.
She imitated the dancers. She waved her
arms. She pointed her toes. She tilted
her head. She tripped over the cat.

"*Merwow!*"

"Sorry, Pavlova," said Sadie.
"I guess I need to practise more."

Sadie practised in the kitchen.

"Mom," she said, "may I go to ballet school?"

Mom said, "Oh, Sadie, wouldn't it be more fun to go to clown school?"

Sadie frowned. "But I don't want to be a clown. I want to be a ballerina."

"We'll see," said Mom.

"We'll see" were Sadie's least favourite words.

One day Sadie saw a poster at the bus stop. The big letters said *The National Ballet Presents The Nutcracker.* Below the letters was a picture of a ballerina.

"That's the Sugar Plum Fairy," said Mom.

Sadie posed on her toes.

She tipped over.

"I wish we could see the Sugar Plum Fairy,"
said Sadie as their bus arrived.

Mom waved her magic shopping bag.
"Abracadabra, your wish shall be granted."

On the bus they sat on the side seats. Sadie stuck out her legs, pointed her toes and let her feet dance in the air. It wasn't easy to dance in running shoes. Even in the air.

People stared. Sadie didn't care.

"It's our stop," said Mom.

Sadie stood up, smiled at the passengers and curtsied.

When they got off the bus Sadie ran ahead.
She leapt and twirled. She waved her
arms. She tilted her head. She bumped
into Mr. Chow who lived next door.

"Oops, sorry, Mr. Chow. I was practising.
I'm going to be a ballerina."

Mr. Chow smiled. "It was my fault, Sadie.
I didn't look where I was going."

Dad was home. Sadie couldn't wait to tell him the news.

"Dad, we're going to the ballet. We're going to see the Sugar Plum Fairy."

"Great," said Dad. "I'll dust off my tux and white necktie."

The evening of the ballet Mom wore a black silk dress. Dad's tux and necktie looked a bit tight. Sadie wore a purple velvet dress with matching silk slippers.

48

The theatre lobby glittered with chandeliers and rhinestones. It smelled of perfume. "*Whoosh,*" said a dress as it swept by, trailing a feather boa. Sadie reached out to stroke the feathers. They disappeared into the crowd.

Sadie's family had front row seats. The musicians in the orchestra pit began to tune their instruments. Sadie stretched out her legs. She pointed her toes and danced in the air. Silk slippers were better for dancing than runners.

Sadie looked at the stage. She wondered
if the Sugar Plum Fairy was hiding
behind the curtain.

Suddenly the music began. The lights
went down, the curtain went up and
Sadie gasped. Everything was so twinkly!

5

"Where's the fairy?" asked Sadie.

"*Shh,*" said Mom.

"*Shh,*" said Dad.

"*Shh,*" said the people behind them.

Finally, the Sugar Plum Fairy entered. She wore a pink tutu and matching satin slippers. "Almost like mine!" said Sadie.

"*Shshsh!*" said everyone.

The fairy sparkled and spun.
She tippytoed and flew right into
the arms of the Nutcracker Prince.

It was just too much for Sadie.

Mom was the first to notice. Sadie's seat was empty. "Where's Sadie?" she whispered to Dad.

"I don't know," Dad whispered back.

They looked right. They looked left. They looked down. They looked up. They gasped. Sadie was on stage.

She was running toward the
Sugar Plum Fairy. The Sugar
Plum Fairy looked surprised.

Mom slid down in her seat.
Dad slid down in his seat.
"Oh, Sadie," they whispered.

The Sugar Plum Fairy didn't miss a beat. She stepped forward, arms outstretched, picked up Sadie and spun her in the air. Sadie was flying.

"What's your name?" asked the fairy.

"Sadie," said Sadie.

"I'm the Sugar Plum Fairy," said the Sugar Plum Fairy. Then she winked and handed Sadie to the Nutcracker.

The Nutcracker Prince lifted
Sadie into the air. Sadie gracefully
waved her arms and pointed her
toes and tilted her head.

Then the Nutcracker handed her down to the harpist. The harpist handed her to the first violin. The first violin handed her to the conductor. The conductor handed her to Mom.

Mom plopped her in her seat.

"Stay put, Sadie," she said. This time Sadie stayed put.

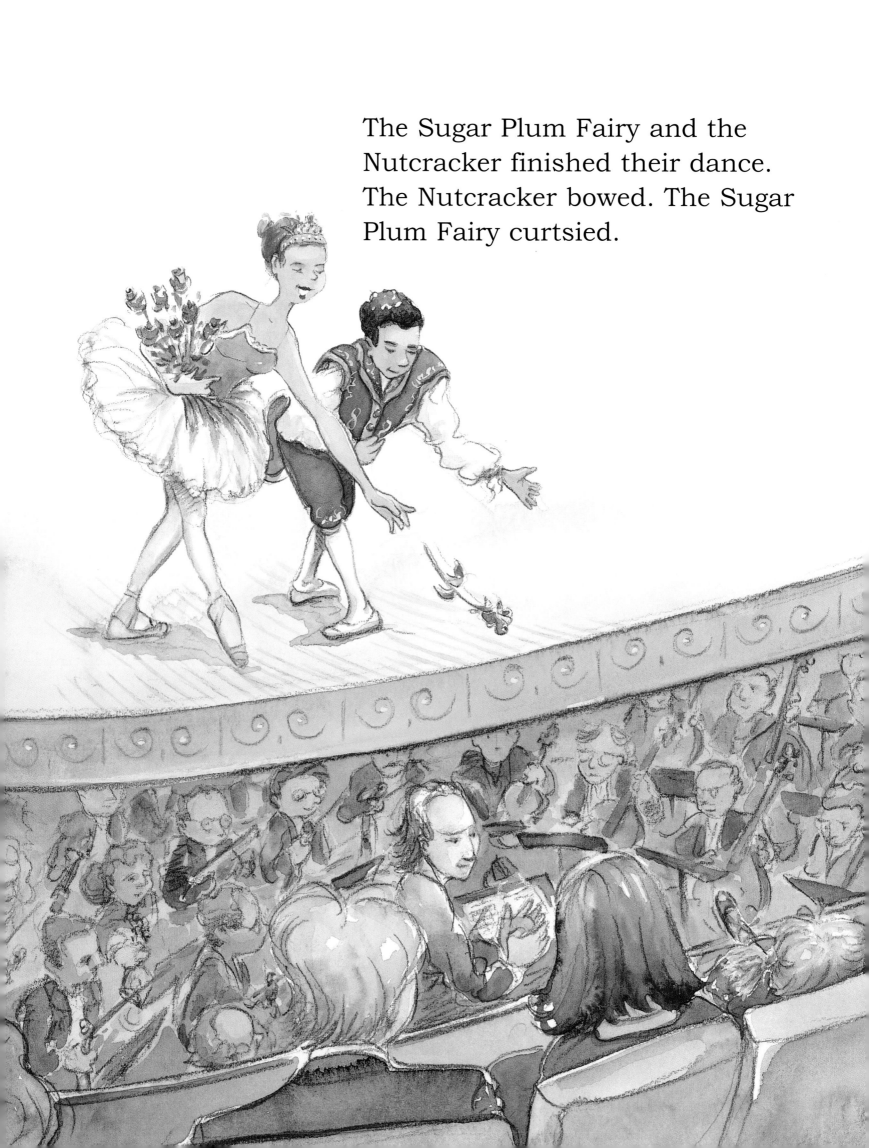

The Sugar Plum Fairy and the Nutcracker finished their dance. The Nutcracker bowed. The Sugar Plum Fairy curtsied.

At the curtain call someone handed
a bouquet of roses to the Sugar Plum Fairy.
She plucked out a rose and tossed it into
Sadie's lap. Sadie blushed.

Back in the lobby one of the ushers handed Mom a note. She read it out loud. "Sadie's a natural, but she needs a little practice. I highly recommend ballet school! Love from the Sugar Plum Fairy."

Sadie looked up at her mom. "May I? Please?"

Mom waved her magic evening purse.
"Abracadabra, your wish is granted."

Sadie waved her arms. She pointed her toes.
She tilted her head. She didn't trip.

People stared but Sadie didn't care.

She was going to be a ballerina.

MOON and STAR
A Christmas Story

Robin Muller

To Samantha Youssef,
the angel at the top of the
Christmas tree

and to
Chip Jones,
a dear friend and
patient adviser.

MOON and STAR

A Christmas Story

Robin Muller

Long ago, in a shop filled with toys, there lived a dog. He was large and gentle, with a moon-shaped mark around his eye. The old lady who owned the shop called him Moon.

Moon loved all the toys, but secretly he loved one above all the others: a delicate little porcelain cat with a shining star painted on its face. Moon called the cat Star, and he wanted her to be his alone. Every night, after the old lady had gone to bed, Moon would carry Star to his mat by the stove. There he would curl himself around her and go happily to sleep, always making sure she was back on the shelf before the old lady rose in the morning.

As Christmas drew near, the old lady bubbled with ideas for the shop's window. She finally decided on a tree adorned with all of her most cherished toys. A tree was ordered, and when it arrived, the old lady set to work, decorating it branch by branch till it was almost finished. All that was needed was the toy that would sit at the top.

There she placed a beautiful doll with rosy cheeks, sparkling black eyes and a cape that shimmered like spun gold.

"When I was a girl," the old lady told Moon, "it was said that the toy that stood at the top of the tree watched over all the other toys, making sure they went to the ones who would love them best."

Moon wagged his tail and, while the old lady was lighting the Christmas candles, he hid Star among the branches. He knew that Star would be his, since no one could love the little porcelain cat more.

The tree in the shop window attracted so many customers that by late afternoon on Christmas Eve nearly all the toys had been sold. The old lady was preparing to close when a huge automobile rolled up. A richly dressed woman stepped out and entered the shop. She strode around, viewing the remaining toys with disdain.

"No, no, no," she said, and was turning to leave when she spotted Star nestled in the tree's boughs. "That little cat is exactly what I'm looking for," she cried. "I must have it!"

Moon began barking frantically.

"What an annoying animal," snorted the woman. "Remove it at once!"

"He's usually so friendly," said the old lady as she dragged Moon to the storeroom and shut him in. "I don't know what's got into him."

Then she put the little porcelain cat in a box, tied it with a ribbon, and gave it to the woman.

The moment Moon was freed he rushed out to the street, but the automobile was gone. With his nose to the ground, Moon followed the scent. He followed it for hours till, far out in the countryside, he came to a long driveway at the end of which stood a magnificent house. Cautiously he crept up and looked through a window into a lighted room. There he saw an enormous Christmas tree, the woman, and a little boy.

The boy sat surrounded by a jumble of opened boxes, all of which contained various articles of clothing. The look of disappointment on his face made Moon feel very sad.

The woman also saw the boy's unhappiness and, with a hearty "Merry Christmas," gave him the box from the toyshop. Eagerly the boy tore off the ribbon and opened the lid. His face beamed with happiness as he lifted the little porcelain cat into the light.

Moon suddenly felt very selfish for wanting to keep Star all to himself. Maybe she was meant for the little boy.

Moon turned to go. He paused to take one last look back. The little boy's smile of delight was gone, replaced by a puzzled frown as he turned the cat over and over.

"But what does it do?" he asked. "Bob its head? Swish its tail? Meow?"

"It does absolutely nothing," replied the woman. "I bought it just because it was pretty."

At this the boy's frown became an angry glare. Moon watched in horror as he hurled Star against a wall, smashing the cat into pieces.

Tears poured from Moon's eyes as a maid swept the pieces into the box and carried them from the room. He raced around to the rear of the house and waited. Soon the maid appeared and tossed the box onto a rubbish heap. Rushing forward, Moon nosed off the lid. He let out a howl of grief at the sight of the shattered remains of his friend.

Heartbroken, Moon replaced the lid and, carefully holding the box in his jaws, began the long journey home. The snow, which had been falling gently, now turned into a blizzard. Freezing winds and gusts of snow battered him till he was so tired that he could walk no farther. Moon curled himself around the box and fell asleep.

As he slept, the storm ended and the sky cleared. Stars twinkled above as a wondrous silence filled the night, a silence broken only by the soft footfall of someone approaching.

A beautiful woman with rosy cheeks, sparkling black eyes and a cape that shimmered like spun gold came toward him. Without disturbing Moon, she brushed the snow from the box and looked in. Gently she gathered the pieces of the broken cat into her hands and held them to her heart. For a moment all the stars in the night sky seemed to blaze. Then she returned the pieces to the box, replaced the lid and continued on her way.

Moon woke to the sound of bells. It was Christmas morning. He shook off the snow, picked up the box, and resumed his journey back to the toyshop. When he finally came to the door, the old lady was overjoyed. She started to put her arms around him, but the sorrow in his eyes stopped her.

Moon walked slowly to his mat by the stove, put down the box, and curled himself around it.

"What do you have there?" the old lady asked softly, and lifted the lid.

"Bless me," she cried in surprise, "she looks just like that little porcelain cat!"

In the box was a real live kitten with a star-shaped mark on her face. Moon sniffed the kitten and barked for joy. His precious Star was whole again.

Together they lived happily in the toyshop.
As the years went by Star had kittens of her own,
all with shining stars on their faces. Each night,
when Moon and Star went to sleep, the kittens
would come and curl themselves around the pair
till, in the silvery light, they looked as if they
were cradled by all the stars in heaven.

One Special Tree

Dedicated to my parents, Roman and Marika Kassian,
who provided the models for the thoughtful
mother and father in this book.

I'll never forget the Christmas of The Tree.

It started out like any other Christmas. Outside, a deep quilting of snow made the world seem quiet and peaceful. Inside, our excitement was growing. There was so much to do, and so much to look forward to! Like buying our tree.

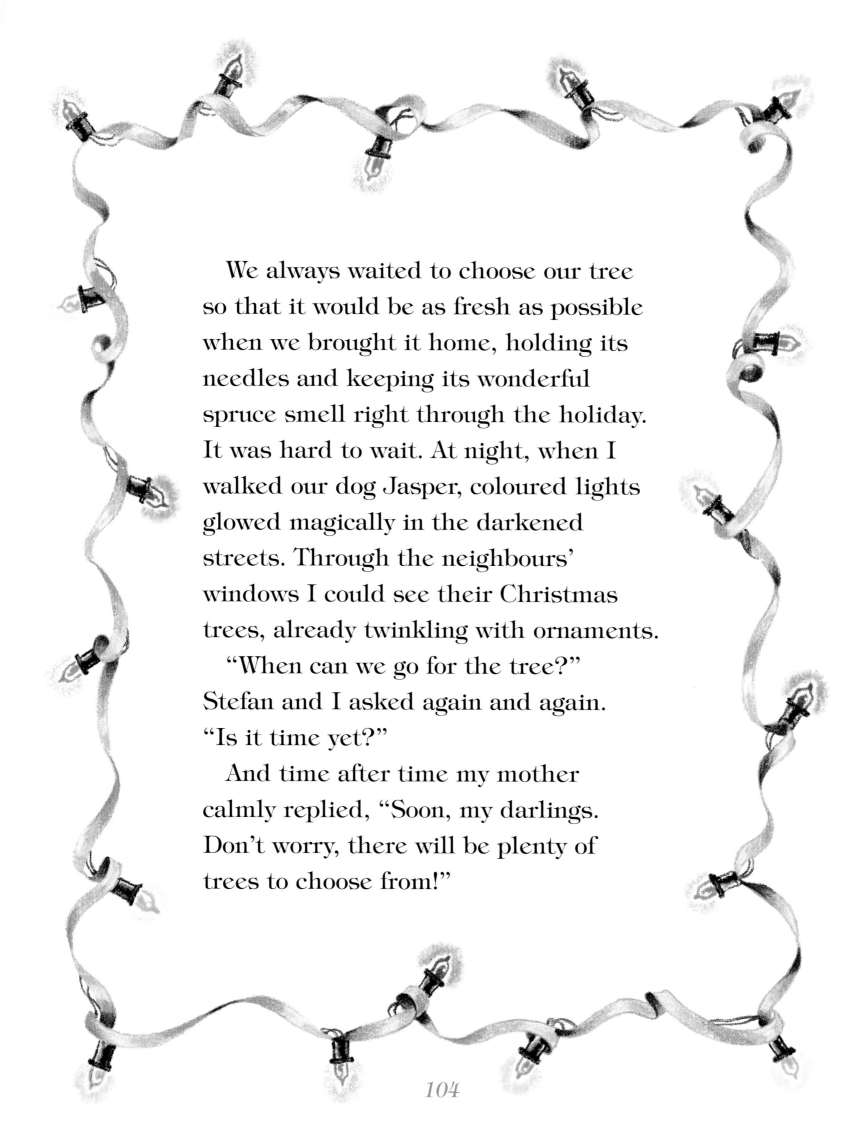

We always waited to choose our tree so that it would be as fresh as possible when we brought it home, holding its needles and keeping its wonderful spruce smell right through the holiday. It was hard to wait. At night, when I walked our dog Jasper, coloured lights glowed magically in the darkened streets. Through the neighbours' windows I could see their Christmas trees, already twinkling with ornaments.

"When can we go for the tree?" Stefan and I asked again and again. "Is it time yet?"

And time after time my mother calmly replied, "Soon, my darlings. Don't worry, there will be plenty of trees to choose from!"

I passed the corner lot every day on my
way home from school, and peered through
the fence at the trees for sale there. Some
were so big they would have filled our small
living room, others so tall they could have
pierced the ceiling. But I knew there was one
among them that would be just right for us.
There always was.

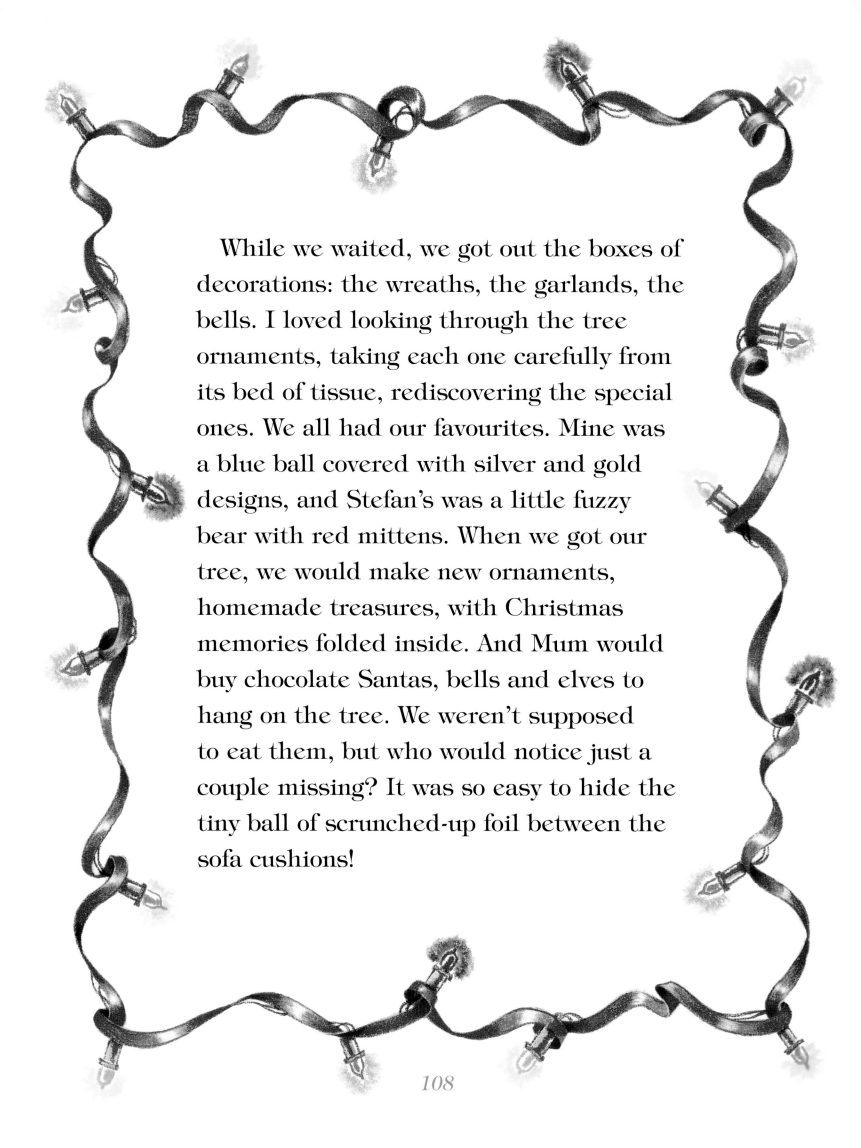

While we waited, we got out the boxes of decorations: the wreaths, the garlands, the bells. I loved looking through the tree ornaments, taking each one carefully from its bed of tissue, rediscovering the special ones. We all had our favourites. Mine was a blue ball covered with silver and gold designs, and Stefan's was a little fuzzy bear with red mittens. When we got our tree, we would make new ornaments, homemade treasures, with Christmas memories folded inside. And Mum would buy chocolate Santas, bells and elves to hang on the tree. We weren't supposed to eat them, but who would notice just a couple missing? It was so easy to hide the tiny ball of scrunched-up foil between the sofa cushions!

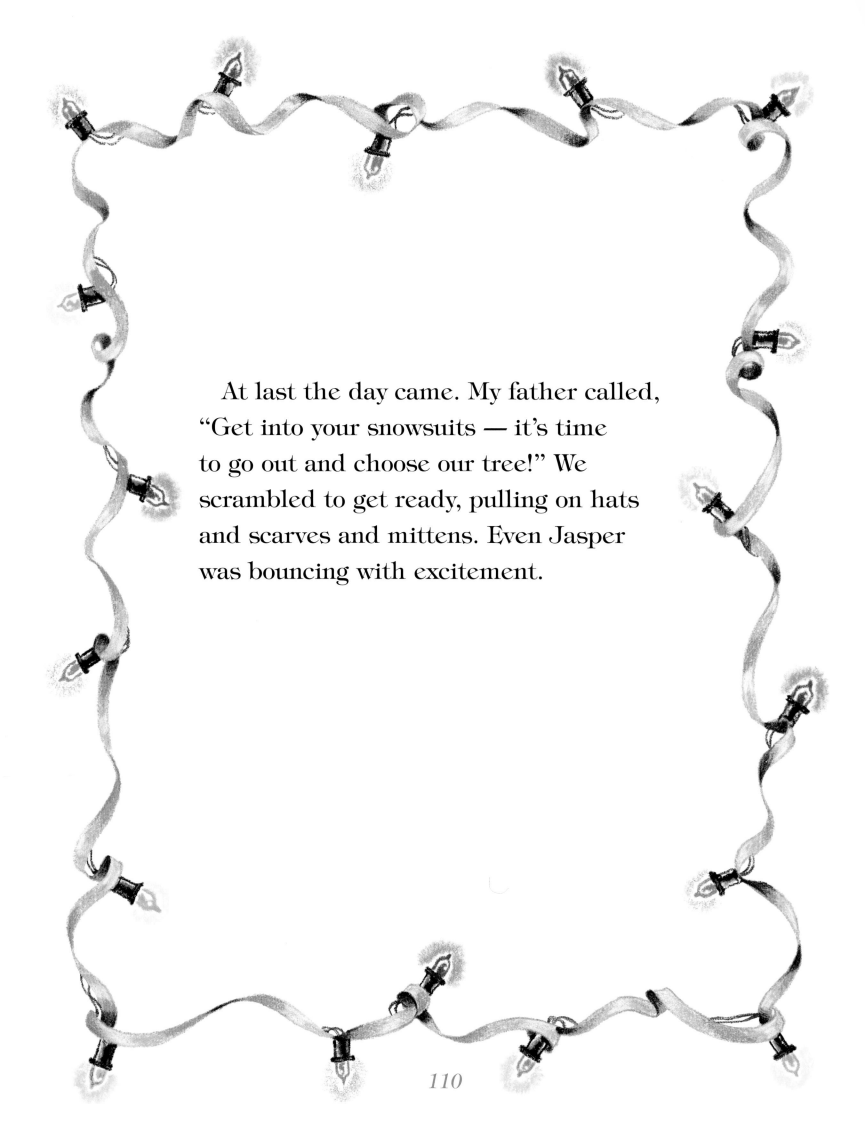

At last the day came. My father called,
"Get into your snowsuits — it's time
to go out and choose our tree!" We
scrambled to get ready, pulling on hats
and scarves and mittens. Even Jasper
was bouncing with excitement.

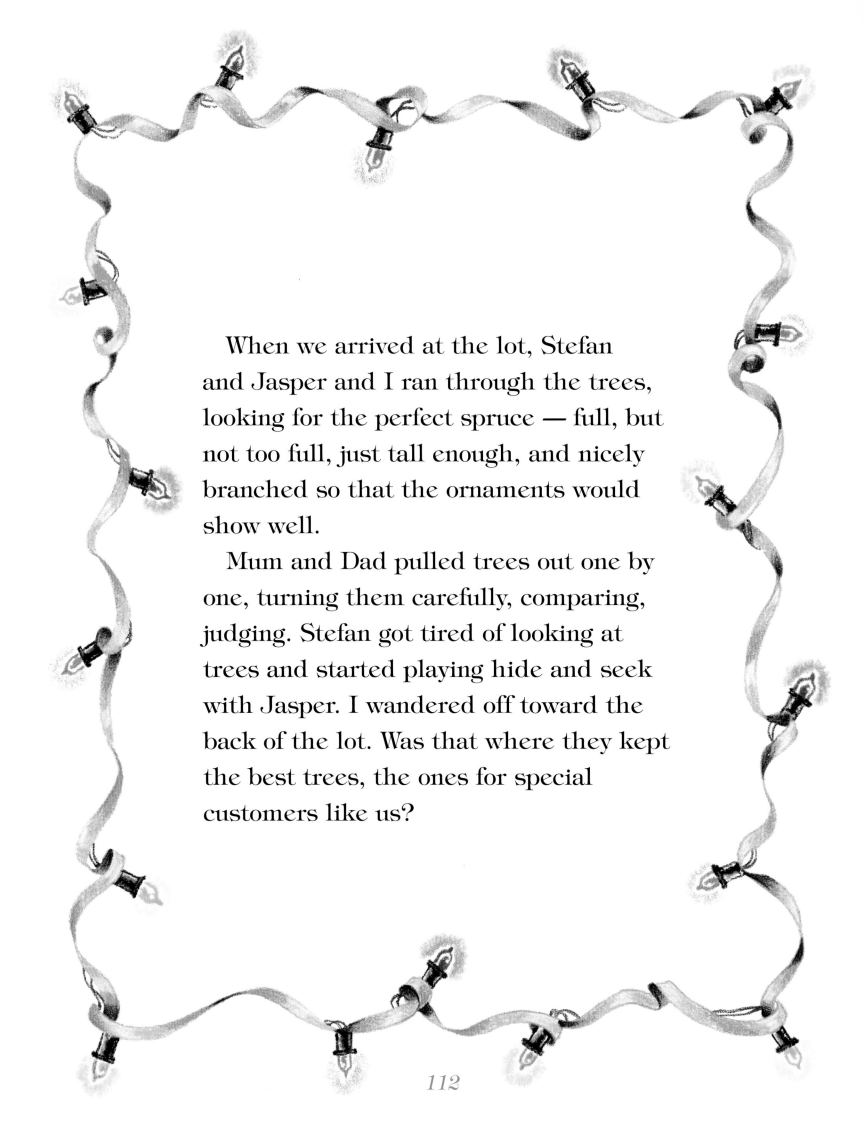

When we arrived at the lot, Stefan and Jasper and I ran through the trees, looking for the perfect spruce — full, but not too full, just tall enough, and nicely branched so that the ornaments would show well.

Mum and Dad pulled trees out one by one, turning them carefully, comparing, judging. Stefan got tired of looking at trees and started playing hide and seek with Jasper. I wandered off toward the back of the lot. Was that where they kept the best trees, the ones for special customers like us?

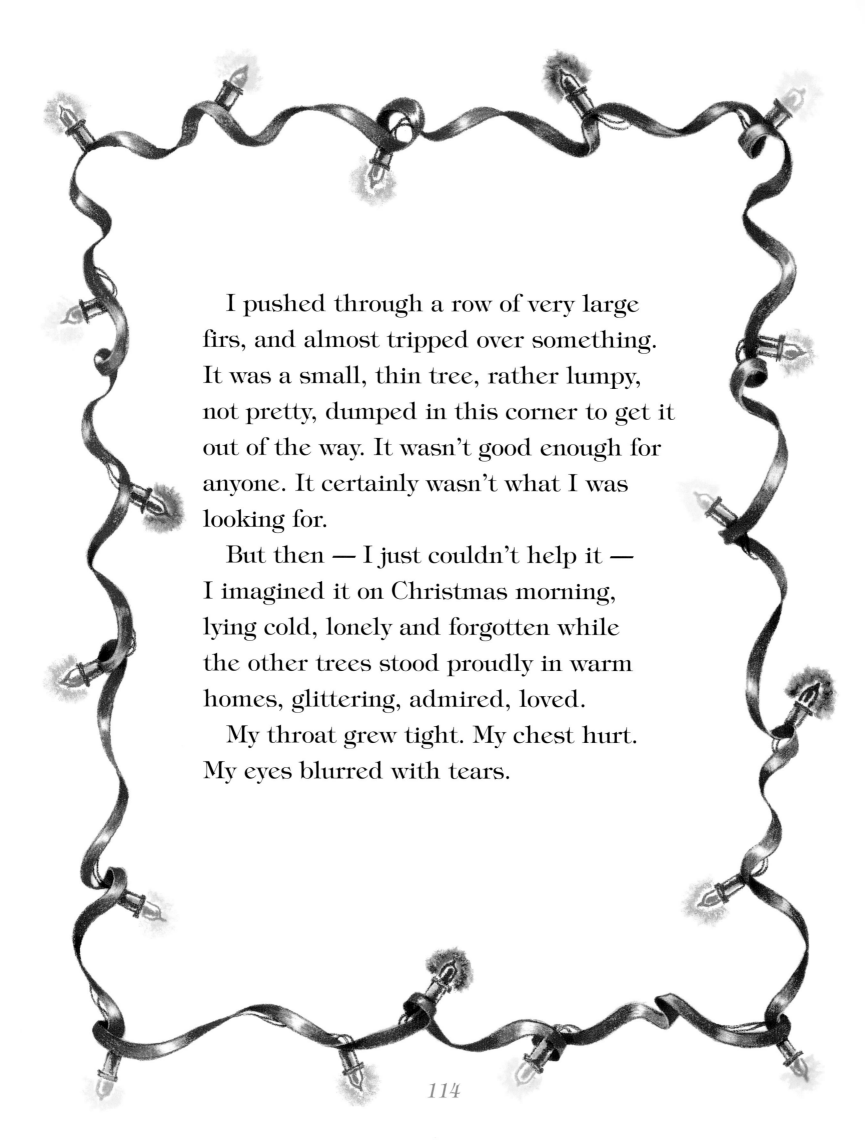

I pushed through a row of very large firs, and almost tripped over something. It was a small, thin tree, rather lumpy, not pretty, dumped in this corner to get it out of the way. It wasn't good enough for anyone. It certainly wasn't what I was looking for.

But then — I just couldn't help it — I imagined it on Christmas morning, lying cold, lonely and forgotten while the other trees stood proudly in warm homes, glittering, admired, loved.

My throat grew tight. My chest hurt. My eyes blurred with tears.

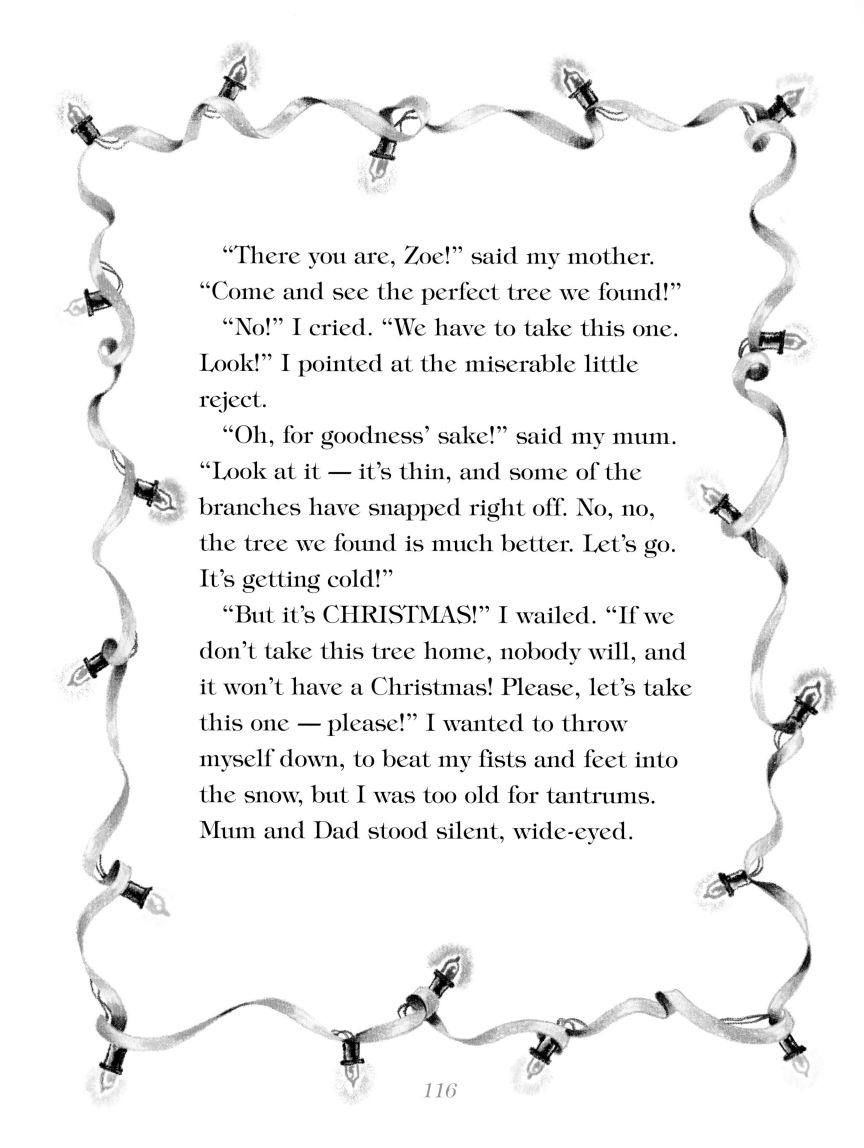

"There you are, Zoe!" said my mother. "Come and see the perfect tree we found!"

"No!" I cried. "We have to take this one. Look!" I pointed at the miserable little reject.

"Oh, for goodness' sake!" said my mum. "Look at it — it's thin, and some of the branches have snapped right off. No, no, the tree we found is much better. Let's go. It's getting cold!"

"But it's CHRISTMAS!" I wailed. "If we don't take this tree home, nobody will, and it won't have a Christmas! Please, let's take this one — please!" I wanted to throw myself down, to beat my fists and feet into the snow, but I was too old for tantrums. Mum and Dad stood silent, wide-eyed.

Then my brother said, in a small voice, "I want Zoe's tree, too."

There was a long pause. I held my breath.

"It seems we've found our Christmas tree, then," Dad said, and picked it up. I took Stefan's hand and sniffed back my tears.

It was dark when we got home, and I felt very tired. Stefan and I got into our pajamas while Mum and Dad set up the tree in the living room.

"How does it look?" I asked, when Mum and Dad came to tuck me in.

My parents looked at each other.

"Christmas trees always look better when they've had time to settle their branches," said Dad, kissing my forehead.

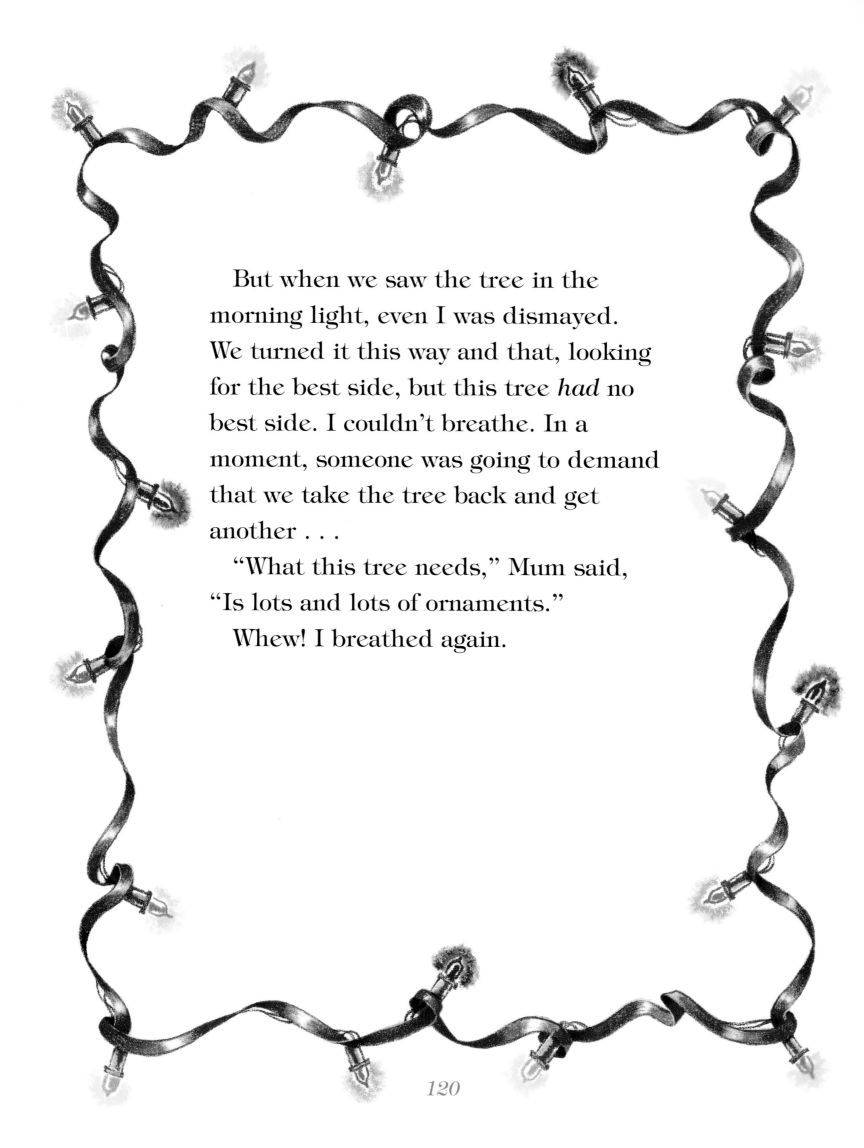

But when we saw the tree in the
morning light, even I was dismayed.
We turned it this way and that, looking
for the best side, but this tree *had* no
best side. I couldn't breathe. In a
moment, someone was going to demand
that we take the tree back and get
another . . .

"What this tree needs," Mum said,
"Is lots and lots of ornaments."

Whew! I breathed again.

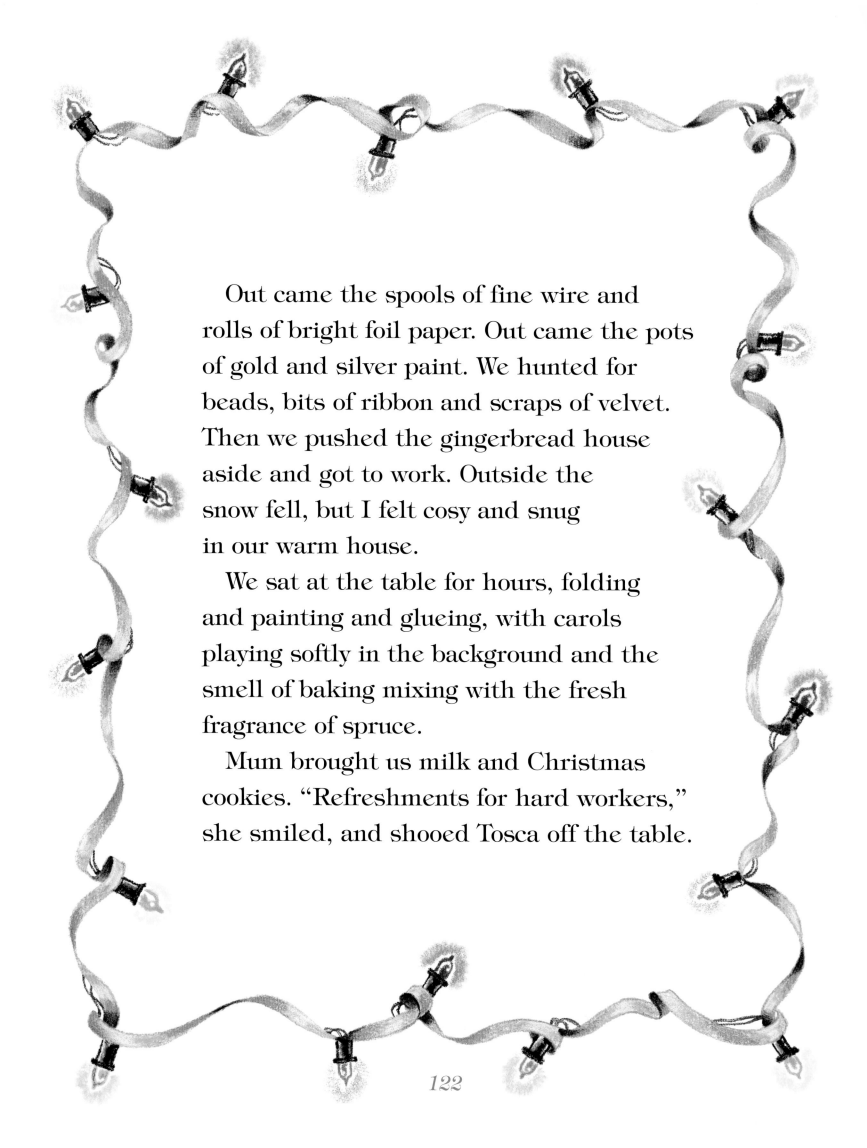

Out came the spools of fine wire and
rolls of bright foil paper. Out came the pots
of gold and silver paint. We hunted for
beads, bits of ribbon and scraps of velvet.
Then we pushed the gingerbread house
aside and got to work. Outside the
snow fell, but I felt cosy and snug
in our warm house.

We sat at the table for hours, folding
and painting and glueing, with carols
playing softly in the background and the
smell of baking mixing with the fresh
fragrance of spruce.

Mum brought us milk and Christmas
cookies. "Refreshments for hard workers,"
she smiled, and shooed Tosca off the table.

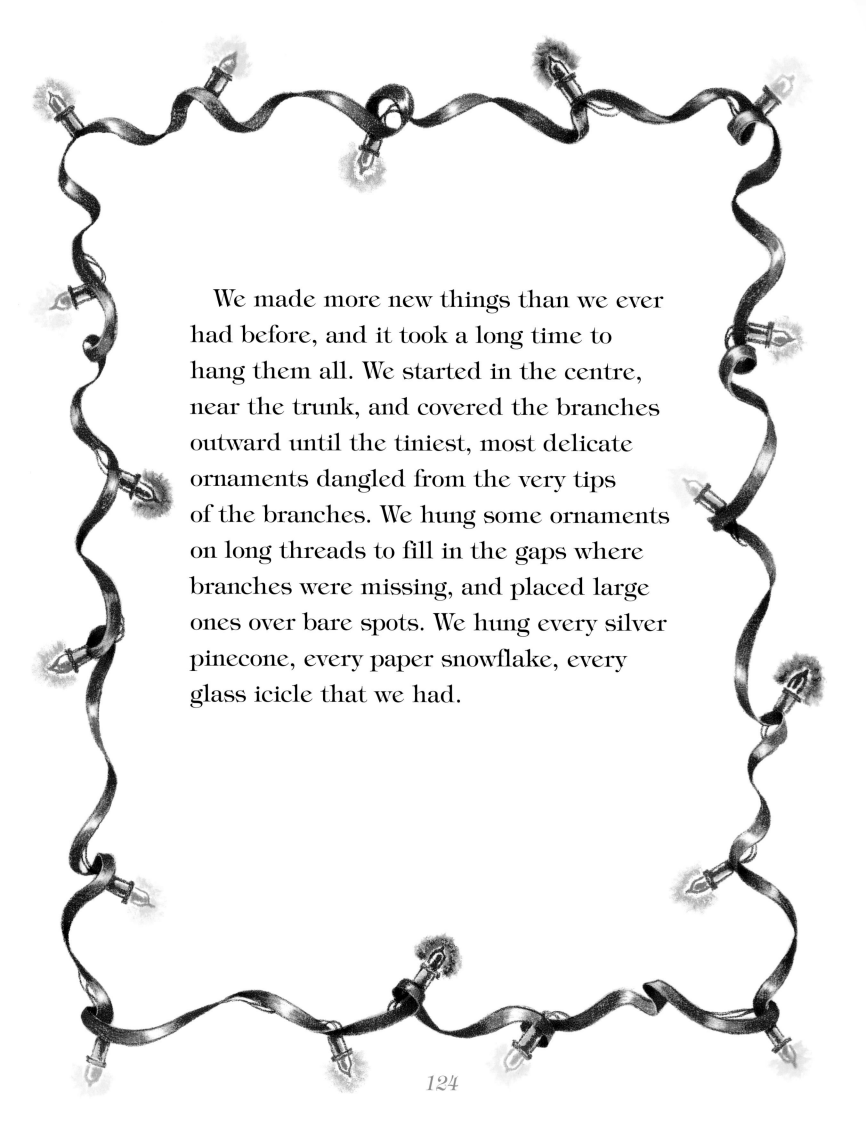

We made more new things than we ever had before, and it took a long time to hang them all. We started in the centre, near the trunk, and covered the branches outward until the tiniest, most delicate ornaments dangled from the very tips of the branches. We hung some ornaments on long threads to fill in the gaps where branches were missing, and placed large ones over bare spots. We hung every silver pinecone, every paper snowflake, every glass icicle that we had.

Only one thing was left.

"Hey!" Stefan said. "We can't put the star on top!" He held it up, the old gold star that had crowned every one of our Christmas trees forever. "There's no tip for it to sit on!"

No gold star? We tried and tried, but we couldn't make it fit. What good were all our efforts, without that final touch? My brother slumped at the table.

Then he sat straight up again and reached for the gingerbread house. He carried it to my dad, who balanced it carefully on the tree's flat top. Mum added a wide velvet ribbon, and we stood back to look.

Who would have thought it? It worked!

Our special tree was finished.
It wasn't perfect, but oh, it was BEAUTIFUL!

How to make Zoe and Stefan's Snowflake Ornament

Materials:

Wrapping or craft paper

Ruler

Scissors

Stapler

Tape

- Cut a piece of paper about 18 x 30 cm (heavy foil wrapping paper works well).

- On the short side, make a fold about 2 cm deep. Continue to fold, accordion-style, until the whole paper is folded. If you're using wrapping paper, the coloured side should show on both sides — if you have extra paper, trim it off.

- Fold the accordion in half, to make a crease.

- Put a staple along the crease.

- Now cut 2 or 3 small triangles into each folded side of the accordion, on both sides of the staple, to make your snowflake. Don't cut too much away, or your snowflake will fall apart.

- Trim the ends at an angle.

- Gently open the snowflake into a circle and tape the open edges together on the back of the snowflake.

- Thread a ribbon or string through one of the holes, and your snowflake is ready to hang on the tree!

Tip:
If you make the same pattern of cuts on both sides of the staple, your snowflake will be symmetrical like a real snowflake.

Frances Tyrrell

Woodland Christmas
Twelve Days of Christmas
in the
North Woods

For our little cub, Neil.

The animals in this book are:
one gray partridge,
two rock doves, three ruffed grouse,
four common loons, five river otters,
six Canada geese, seven whistling swans, eight raccoons,
nine red foxes, ten moose, eleven red squirrels
and twelve beavers.
The bird in the potted pear tree
is a California partridge,
and the courting couple are black bears.

Frances Tyrrell

Woodland Christmas

Twelve Days of Christmas
in the
North Woods

On the first day of Christmas,
My true love gave to me
A partridge in a pear tree.

On the second day of Christmas,
My true love gave to me:
Two turtledoves
And a partridge in a pear tree.

On the third day of Christmas,
My true love gave to me:
Three French hens
Two turtledoves
And a partridge in a pear tree.

On the fourth day of Christmas,
My true love gave to me:
Four calling birds
Three French hens
Two turtledoves
And a partridge in a pear tree.

On the fifth day of Christmas,
My true love gave to me:
Five golden rings
Four calling birds
Three French hens
Two turtledoves
And a partridge in a pear tree.

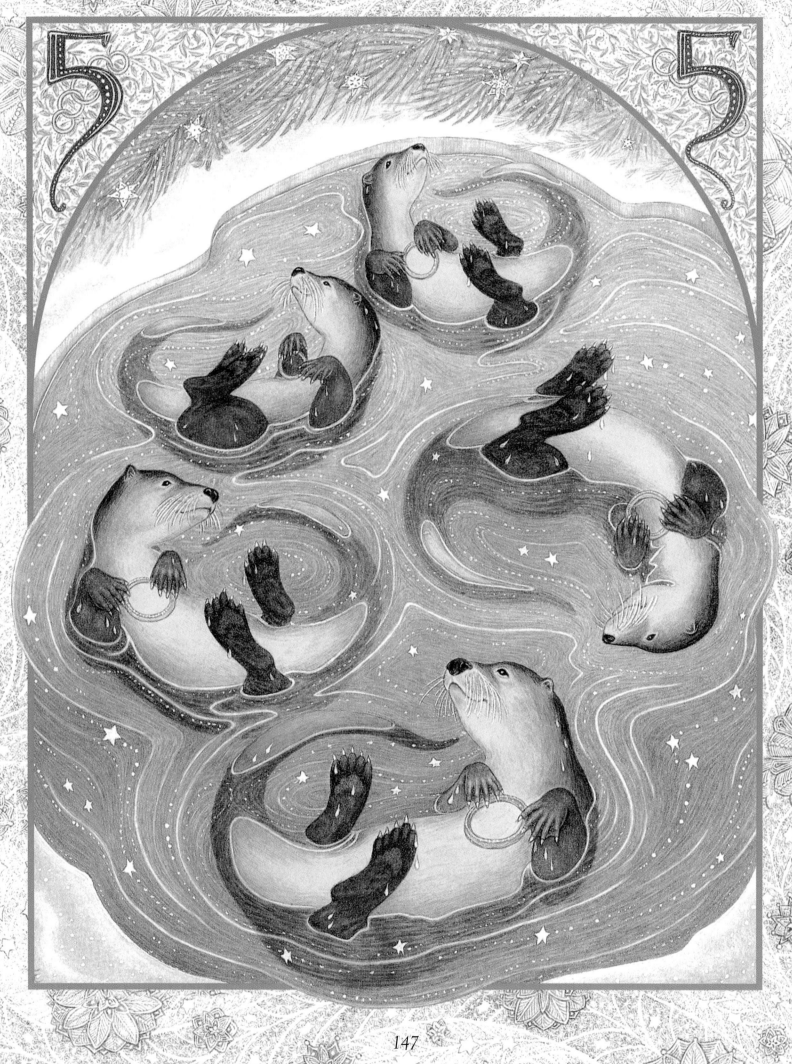

On the sixth day of Christmas,
My true love gave to me:
Six geese a-laying
Five golden rings
Four calling birds
Three French hens
Two turtledoves
And a partridge in a pear tree.

On the seventh day of Christmas,
My true love gave to me:
Seven swans a-swimming
Six geese a-laying
Five golden rings
Four calling birds
Three French hens
Two turtledoves
And a partridge in a pear tree.

On the eighth day of Christmas,
My true love gave to me:
Eight maids a-milking
Seven swans a-swimming
Six geese a-laying
Five golden rings
Four calling birds
Three French hens
Two turtledoves
And a partridge in a pear tree.

On the ninth day of Christmas,
My true love gave to me:
Nine ladies dancing
Eight maids a-milking
Seven swans a-swimming
Six geese a-laying
Five golden rings
Four calling birds
Three French hens
Two turtledoves
And a partridge in a pear tree.

On the tenth day of Christmas,
My true love gave to me:
Ten lords a-leaping
Nine ladies dancing
Eight maids a-milking
Seven swans a-swimming
Six geese a-laying
Five golden rings
Four calling birds
Three French hens
Two turtledoves
And a partridge in a pear tree.

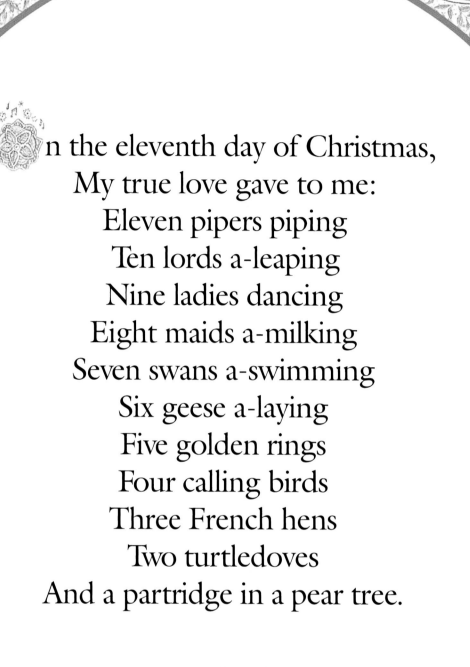

On the eleventh day of Christmas,
My true love gave to me:
Eleven pipers piping
Ten lords a-leaping
Nine ladies dancing
Eight maids a-milking
Seven swans a-swimming
Six geese a-laying
Five golden rings
Four calling birds
Three French hens
Two turtledoves
And a partridge in a pear tree.

On the twelfth day of Christmas,
My true love gave to me:
Twelve drummers drumming
Eleven pipers piping
Ten lords a-leaping
Nine ladies dancing
Eight maids a-milking
Seven swans a-swimming
Six geese a-laying
Five golden rings
Four calling birds
Three French hens
Two turtledoves
And a partridge in a pear tree.

The
Twelve Days of Christmas

About the Authors and Illustrators

Michael Cutting

Michael Cutting was born in England, and was a bit of black sheep from the start: he always had his own way of doing things. His mother died when he was only 10 days old, and he didn't meet his father, a career military officer, until he was a toddler. Until then, he was raised by his paternal grandparents and cousins, whom he loved dearly. He particularly admired his grandfather, who had ridden a penny-farthing bicycle to court his future wife, and who taught young Michael to drive.

When he grew up, Michael served in Her Majesty's Royal Engineers. After military service, he made his way to Canada as a ship's purser for the Cunard line. He had successful careers in advertising and television in Canada and the U.S., and eventually found his way to Oakville, Ontario, where he lived for the rest of his life. He loved his garden, mainly for its ability to attract wild creatures, all of which he named. Animals were his passion, says his daughter Vivienne, and there were always a few around when she was growing up. "One day, he picked me up from a birthday party and there was a tiger cub in the back seat of the car!"

When Michael wrote *The Little Crooked Christmas Tree*, he wanted to create something lasting, the kind of story that families enjoy together every year. And he succeeded — the book has never been out of print, and was made into a television film narrated by Christopher Plummer. Michael died in 2004, but this story remains his lasting Christmas gift to young readers.

Ron Broda

Ron Broda has illustrated many books, but *The Little Crooked Christmas Tree* has a special place in his heart. It was his first book, and its publication was a huge boost; but perhaps it is also because he, too, grew up feeling a little different. Ron struggled in school, with what turned out to be dyslexia. He had many friends and enjoyable days, but "I thought I was stupid," he says, and no one, not even Ron himself, thought he would continue after high school. But one day a perceptive teacher suggested the graphic design program at a nearby college, and there Ron flourished, developing his unique style of paper sculpture.

His work is labour-intensive and time-consuming, "but the first five percent of a book is fun," says Ron. He keeps himself interested by having the TV on in the background, or listening to music or the radio. "The last five percent gets fun again, and then, when the finished book comes in, after you haven't seen it for a while—it's like Christmas!"

What's the first thing that pops into Ron's head when he hears that word? No surprise—it's decorations! Every year the tree has a different theme, and Ron delights in surprising his children with offbeat gifts: five-foot-long trout pillows or freakishly real-looking stuffed baboons. His main enjoyment of the season, however, is in spending time with his family. And every year, they watch *The Little Crooked Christmas Tree* together.

Joan Betty Stuchner

*I*n *Sadie the Ballerina*, a little girl with big dreams makes something happen in an unexpected way. That's real magic, says author Joan Betty Stuchner—though she hasn't stopped hoping that one day, a team of fairies will clean her house from top to bottom in the blink of an eye!

Joan was born in England and came to Canada in the 1960s. She studied English Literature and trained to be a teacher; today, she teaches and works as a library clerk in Vancouver, BC. She danced as a child, and for a surprising reason: her parents hoped it would fix her bow legs. It worked — thanks to the fearsome teacher, who strode around the floor with a big stick, tapping any legs that weren't absolutely straight! Joan enjoyed dancing, but wasn't very good at following directions. She also suffered greatly from stage fright. She still does, but now she uses it to perform better as a stage actor, something she enjoys in her spare time.

And, of course, Joan writes. Some days, it just plods along. Then, a turn of phrase or a certain word will apppear "from nowhere," lifting her writing, twirling it around and setting it down again, with its feet on a new and better path. That, too, says Joan, is magic!

Bruno St-Aubin

A couple of girls he knows inspired the small dancer in *Sadie the Ballerina*, but ballet itself is also inspiring, says illustrator Bruno St-Aubin—both "an art and a sport." An amateur sportsman as a youth, he admires the balanced conditioning of the dancer's body. He doesn't dance himself, but he does run, to make sure that the "*livres*" collect on his shelves and not around his middle!

Bruno discovered his own artistic path bit by bit. He wanted to be a musician, but had more talent for drawing. After a false start in surveying class, he happily moved to graphic design, then illustration. He loves his work — in fact, if he could have a wish granted right now, it would be for a clone Bruno, to do more painting, drawing and school visits! He enjoys that last part of being an illustrator very much. Some encouragement here, a little drawing there — you never know, he says, what kind of quiet magic you do when you interact with children.

He also loves a good surprise. Bruno lives in Montreal, and one morning, he got up early to drive to a small school 100 kilometres away . . . only to find that he was in the wrong place! The startled but very pleased principal organized a special day for him and all the primary students. And, a month later, they invited him back! That kind of mistake, says Bruno, is one of the best gifts of all.

Robin Muller

Why do Christmas and toys belong together? Robin Muller thinks it's because toys speak to us about Christmas things: brightness and optimism, joy and warmth. "Apart from our parents, the toys we cherish are our first sources of comfort and support and friendship," says Robin.

He should know — he has a house full of them. And for *Moon and Star*, he invited all his friends to send photos of or lend him their favourite toys. You can find them in the artwork, tucked into corners or on shelves, along with the Steadfast Tin Soldier, the Velveteen Rabbit, and a host of other famous playthings. You can also find Robin himself, hurrying to his publisher with some finished artwork tucked under his arm. Sadly, Sally, the little dog at his side, is no more.

Would Moon have been just as happy to have Star restored to him as she was, a porcelain cat? Robin thinks so. "When you love someone, you don't care what they are. But as a real cat, Star was able to love him back." Robin lives in Toronto, Ontario, and he still loves Christmas, which he considers a gift in itself. Still, he does secretly wish every year for that special box wrapped in bright paper with a big bow, containing the certain something (he doesn't know what) that will make everything brighter and better!

Olena Kassian

Olena Kassian based her story *One Special Tree* on her own memories of Christmastime. Every year, she looks forward to the fun and closeness of this special time of year. In fact, her favourite gift is the arrival of family members from faraway places. And the best gift she ever gave? A photo album for each of her children, covered in red-and-gold Japanese enamel and filled with memories. Putting them together gave her so much pleasure, she felt like she was giving a gift to herself.

Olena came to Canada with her Ukrainian parents in the 1950s. As a child, her special toys were a collection of horse statues, with which she engaged in many conversations and adventures. She studied art and philosophy at university, drawing and painting at the Ontario College of Art, and has worked in animation, publishing and advertising. "Loblaws is one of my art galleries," she jokes, "with labels for Del Monte, President's Choice, McCain and many others."

Today, Olena focuses on fine art, though she is about to launch a book inspired by the same dog as the one Jasper was based on. She lives in Toronto, and her secret wish for every Christmas is snow — lots and lots of snow. "Canadians complain too much about snow," she says. "It's wonderful!"

Frances Tyrrell

*T*he cozy world illustrator Frances Tyrell created for *Woodland Christmas* was inspired by the nineteenth-century photographs of William Notman, Ontario's cottage country . . . and Canadian woodland creatures, of course. When it came to the eighth day, though, she was stumped: cows didn't fit, and who would dare to milk a moose? Then the resourceful raccoons, with their clever paws and love of shiny things, came to the rescue. About her stately bear family, Frances says: "Good manners are cross-cultural, maybe even cross-species. They are never out of style!"

Frances drew throughout her childhood, doodled through secretarial school, and finally discovered the joys of illustrating. Several of her books have to do with Christmas, a season she describes as "full of magical promise" that never disappoints. (That's pretty much how people describe her artwork, too, which is done in watercolour using a method she developed herself.) The best Christmas present Frances ever received was a set of fine-line Magic Markers when she was twelve. The colours had "proper artist names" — magenta, cerulean, alizarin — which to Frances seemed full of the same magical promise as Christmas itself. It still gives her joy to share that promise in the watercolour classes she teaches in Oakville, Ontario, where she lives with her family.